When Edgar Met Cecil

Kevin

Luthardt

For Elijah and his famous robot. To God be the glory! —K. L.

Published by
PEACHTREE PUBLISHERS
1700 Chattahoochee Avenue
Atlanta, Georgia 30318-2112
www.peachtree-online.com

Illustrations created in acrylic on hot press archival watercolor
paper. Title and text typeset in International Typeface
Corporation's Officina Serif by Erik Spiekermann.

Book design by Loraine M. Joyner and Melanie McMahon Ives

Printed in April 2013 by Imago in China
10 9 8 7 6 5 4 3 2 1
First Edition

Library of Congress Cataloging-in-Publication Data

Luthardt, Kevin.
  When Edgar Met Cecil / by Kevin Luthardt.
       pages cm
  A robot and an alien overcome obstacles to form an unlikely friendship.
  ISBN: 978-1-56145-706-9 / 1-56145-706-X
  [1. Friendship—Fiction. 2. Extraterrestrial beings—Fiction. 3. Robots—Fiction. 4.
Moving, Household—Fiction.] I. Title.
  PZ7.L9793Ed 2013
  [E]—dc23
                         2012032335

Edgar had a nice life.

He loved to play ball with his best pal Quincy.

On the weekends, they watched scary movies.

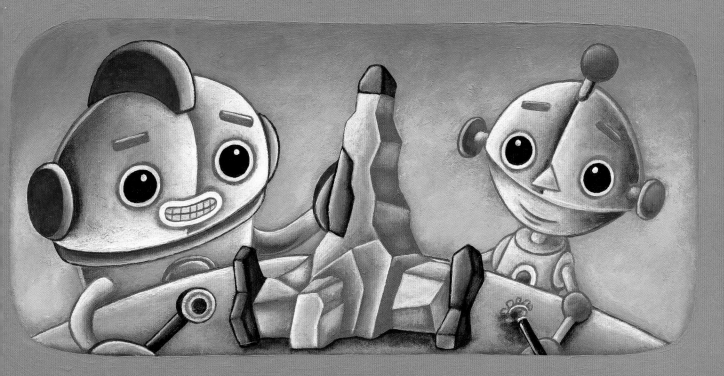

And after school, they liked to build stuff.

One day Edgar's parents told him that they were moving.

Noooooo!

"I can't leave Quincy!" Edgar cried.
"He's my best friend!"

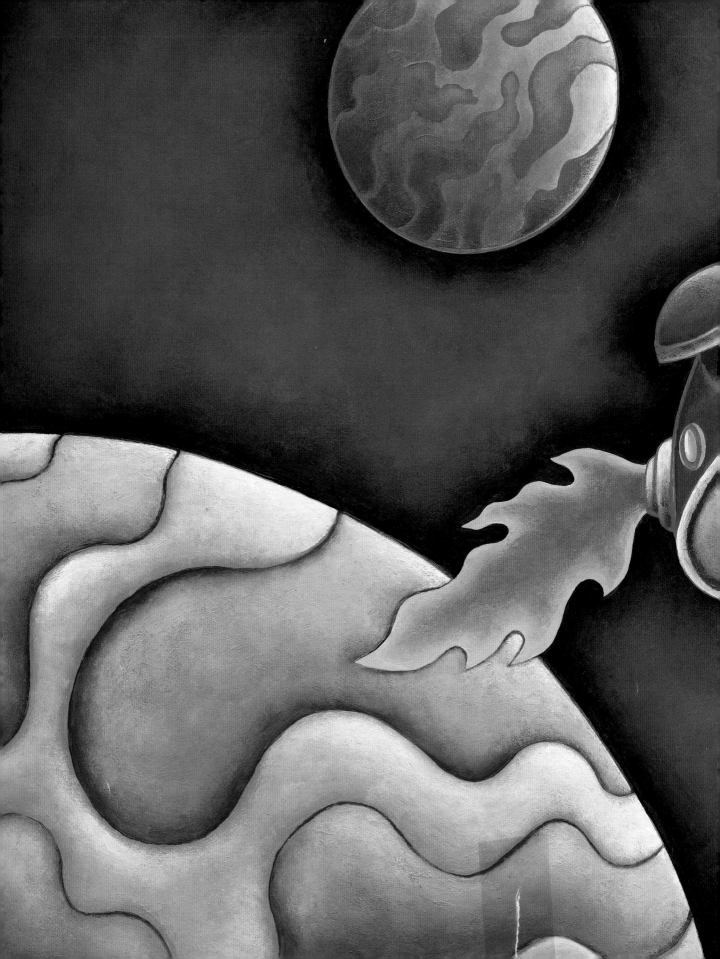

But it was true.

Edgar's family headed off for their new home. He waved goodbye to Quincy and everything he had ever known.

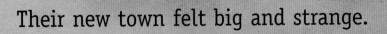

Their new town felt big and strange.

So did Edgar's new school.

Everything was very different.

The kids looked weird.

They dressed funny.

They listened to bizarre music.

They ate strange food.

And the biggest, weirdest kid kept staring at Edgar.

He stood next to Edgar in the cafeteria.

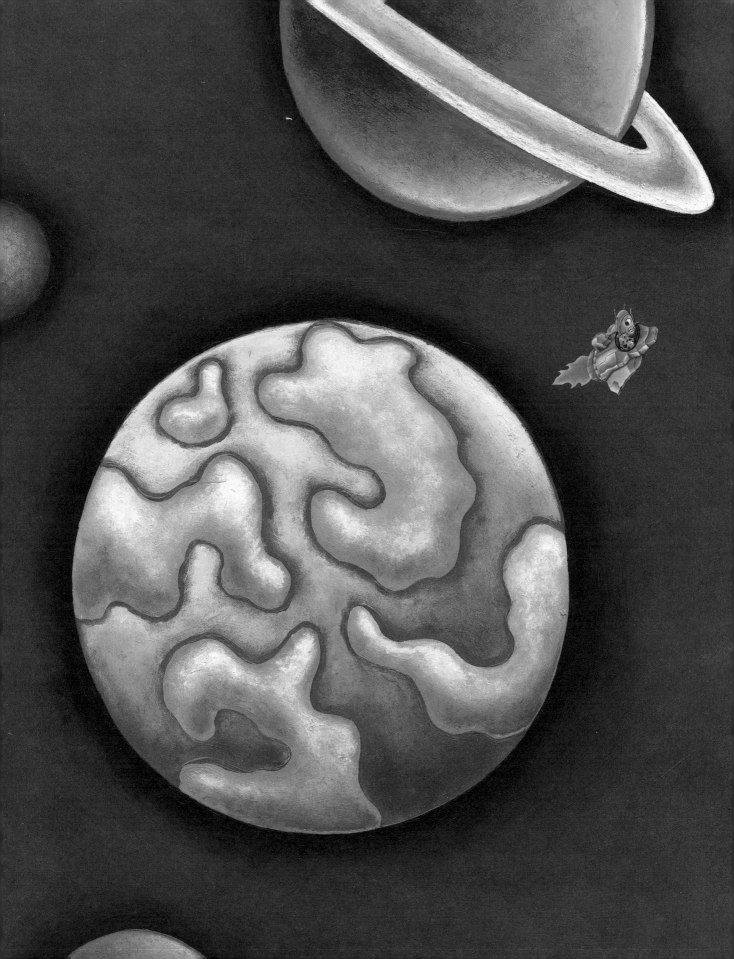

Together, they built something truly amazing!

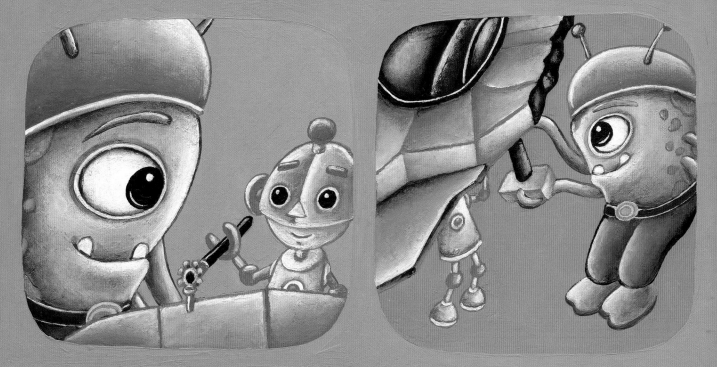

Edgar and Cecil played together for the rest of recess,

and every day after that for the next week.

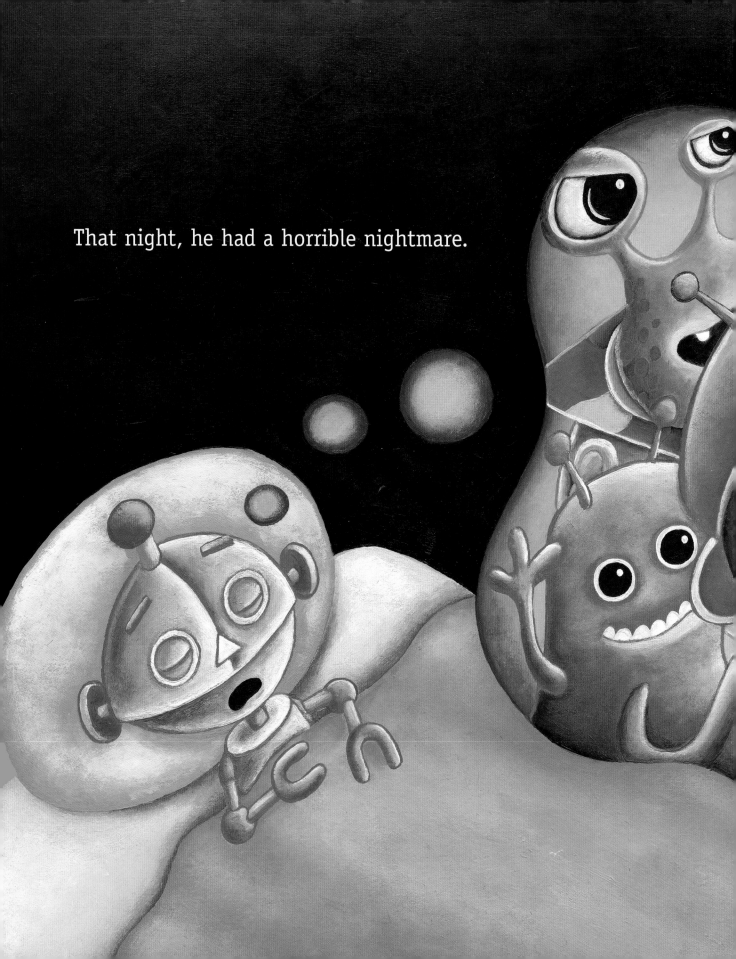

That night, he had a horrible nightmare.

The next day, Edgar
played by himself again.

Suddenly, he realized the big weird kid was heading his way.

"What does he want?" Edgar wondered. "He looks scary."

"You scared me," the big weird kid said. "My name is Cecil."

"Oh… My name is Edgar."

"That's a funny name," Cecil said. "Hey, can I help?"

He sat across from him
in the computer lab.

And he kept an eye on Edgar when they lined up for gym class.

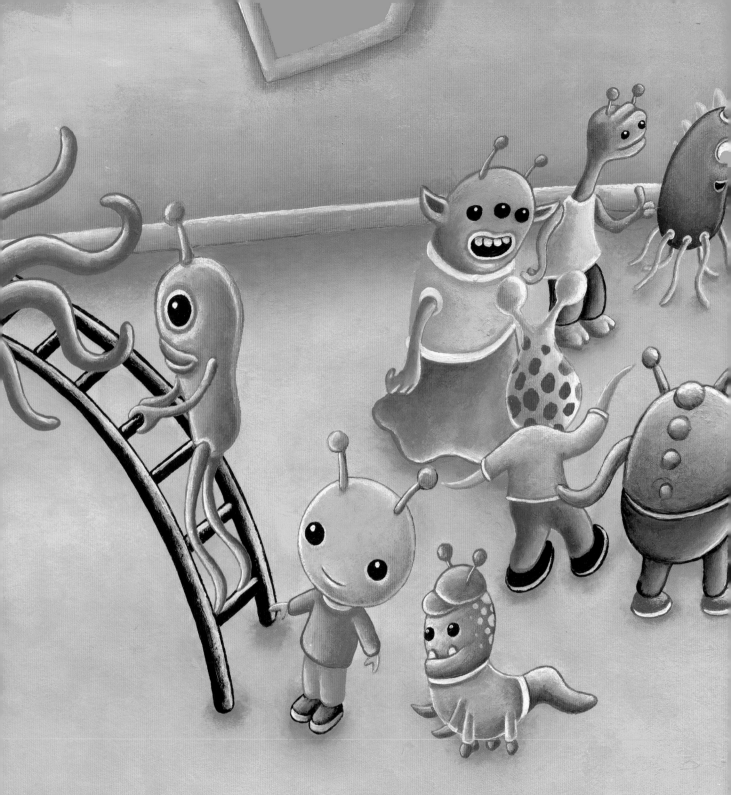

Edgar felt uncomfortable around his new classmates.
At recess, he found a quiet place to play by himself.

He missed Quincy.